ADINKRA SYMBOLS AND THEIR MEANINGS

**dwennimmen
(jin-NEE-meh):**

ram's horns;
means "strength and wisdom"

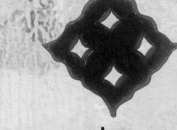

**eban
(eh-BAN):**

fence;
means "safety and security"

**gye nyame
(JEH N-yah-meh):**

most popular Adinkra symbol;
means "faith in and devotion to a supreme being"

**hwemudua
(sheweb-moo-DOO-AH):**

measuring stick;
means "high quality and excellence"

**mate masie
(mah-tee mah-SEE-AH):**

what I hear, I keep;
means "wisdom and knowledge"

**mpuannum
(um-poo-AH-num):**

five tufts of hair;
means "hairstyle of joy
[worn by priestesses] and loyalty"

**pempamsie
(pim-PAHM-see-ah):**

links of a chain;
means "fearlessness"

**sankofa
(san-KO-fah):**

bird looking backward;
means "learn from the past
to build the future"

**sepow
(say-POW):**

dagger;
means "justice and the law"

**wawa aba
(wah-wah AH-bah):**

seed of a wawa tree;
means "toughness
and perseverance"

This book is dedicated to my parents. My mother was a children's librarian and a wonderful writer herself. She read voraciously, especially children's books, and is unequivocally the main reason I am a writer and why this particular book emerged from my heart. My father, a lawyer and a judge, was a patron of the arts and a writer as well. They read to us relentlessly and passed down their staunch belief that words have unmitigated power. May they rest forever in peace and creativity. —T.E.W.

In homage to my loving grandmothers, Ellie and Bessie. You were my foundation. Until we meet again, may you continue to rest in paradise. Your granddaughter —A.H.

A NOTE ABOUT THIS STORY

More than two decades ago, I placed my children in African-centered schools, attracted by those institutions' appreciation for Africa's many diverse cultures. That was also when I initially learned about the Adinkra symbols and their meanings. When I further researched the symbols for this book, I discovered that the interpretations vary from source to source.

Nana Akua Goes to School pays homage to several Ashanti traditions. While the Adinkra symbols and their meanings have been preserved in modern-day Ghana, grandparents and great-grandparents of today's children are the last generations to bear evidence of the tribal marking tradition.

—Tricia Elam Walker

Text copyright © 2020 by Tricia Elam Walker • Jacket art and interior illustrations copyright © 2020 by April Harrison • All rights reserved. Published in the United States by Schwartz & Wade Books, an imprint of Random House Children's Books, a division of Penguin Random House LLC, New York. • Schwartz & Wade Books and the colophon are trademarks of Penguin Random House LLC. • Visit us on the Web! rhcbooks.com • Educators and librarians, for a variety of teaching tools, visit us at RHTeachersLibrarians.com

Library of Congress Cataloging-in-Publication Data is available upon request.
ISBN 978-0-525-58113-0 (hc) • ISBN 978-0-525-58114-7 (lib. bdg.)
ISBN 978-0-525-58115-4 (ebook)

The text of this book is set in Adobe Caslon.
The illustrations were rendered in a mixed-media collage.

MANUFACTURED IN CHINA
10 9 8 7 6 5 4 3 2 1
First Edition

NANA AKUA

GOES TO
SCHOOL

BY **TRICIA ELAM WALKER**

ILLUSTRATED BY **APRIL HARRISON**

schwartz & wade books · new york

It's Circle Time, Zura's favorite time of the day. She scoots to a spot next to Theodore and crisscrosses her legs on the rainbow-shaped rug.

"Ready set?" Mr. Dawson says, looking at the children over his glasses.

"You bet!" they respond, and quiet right down.

"Next Monday is a very important day," Mr. Dawson continues. "Each of you will bring your grandparents to school so they can share what makes them special."

"Yay! Grandparents Day!" shouts Alejo without raising his hand. "My *abuelo* is the best fisherman in the world, and he can explain how to catch the biggest fish!"

Bisou thrusts both hands up and says, "My mimi is the best dentist in the world! She can bring everyone a toothbrush."

All the children chime in, their voices leaping over each other, to tell what's best about their grandparents. "Inside voices, please," says Mr. Dawson.

"What do yours do?" Theodore whispers to Zura.
But Zura just shrugs.

When Zura's *paapa* brings her home from school, Nana Akua, her favorite person in the whole universe, is peeling potatoes for dinner. Although Nana's feet don't even reach the floor, she seems as tall as the giant playground slide. Maybe that's because she's filled to the brim with stories about growing up in West Africa, where people carve statues out of wood, trees drip with mangoes, and crayon-colored outdoor markets sell everything you can imagine.

Nana puts down the peeler and gives Zura one of her
big hugs, the kind that wrap around you like a sweater.

"Grandparents Day is next week," she says.
"Maybe you can help me decide what to talk about."
Zura stares down at the floor.

Zura's *maame* knows about Grandparents Day, too. Her smile is bright as a sunbeam. "How about if Paapa plays the *djembe* drums while Nana talks to your classmates?" she suggests, coming over to help Nana.

Zura frowns and thinks about the last time she and Nana went to the park. Nana pushed her high to the sky on the swings, and Zura was almost flying. But on their way home, a little boy pointed at Nana, and Zura heard him say to his mother, "That lady looks scary."

And the very next day a server in the Little Teahouse stared so hard at Nana, she forgot to bring them sugar cookies with their tea.

This is because Nana Akua looks different. When she was young, her parents followed an old African tradition. They put marks on her face to show which tribal family she belongs to, and to represent beauty and confidence. Those marks never wash off and never go away.

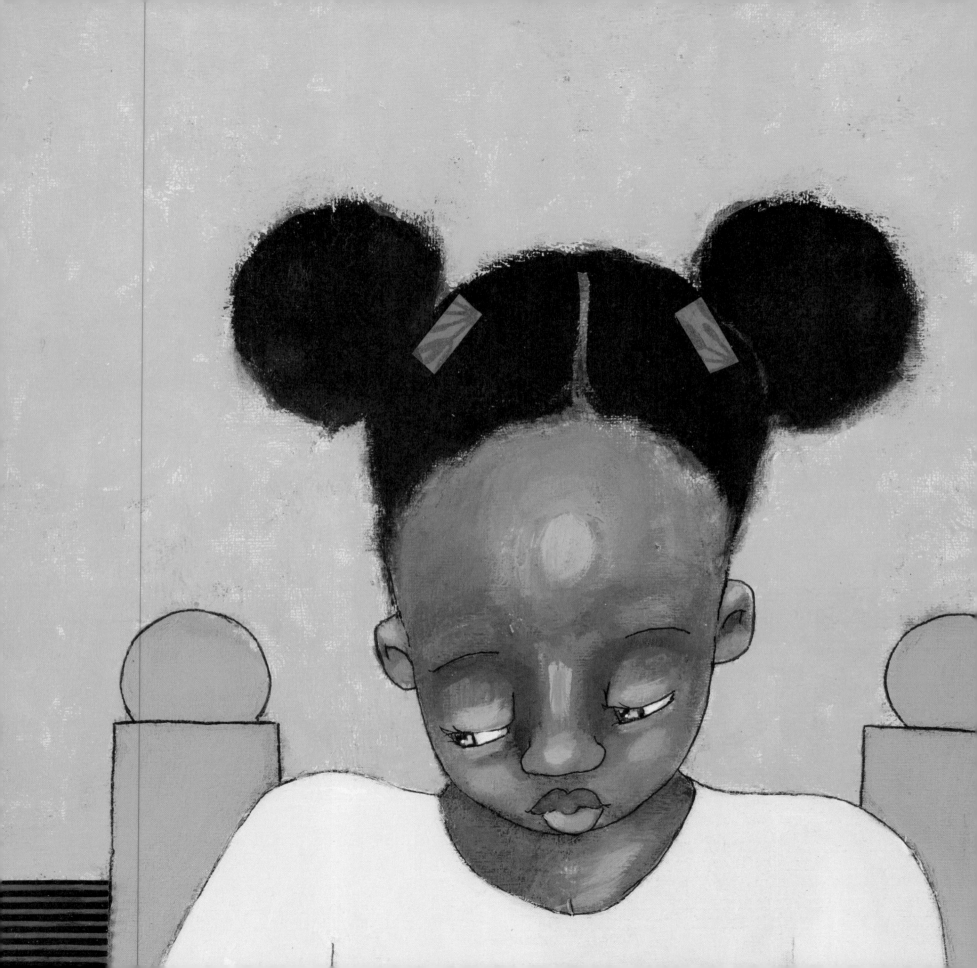

Zura looks at her nana, holding back tears that wait in the corners of her eyes. Nana Akua puts down her potato, takes Zura's hand, and says, "My precious girl, why such a sad face?"

It feels hard to explain, but Zura wants to try. She swallows and takes a deep breath. "What if someone at school laughs at you or acts mean?" she asks quietly.

Nana Akua thinks for a moment. "I have an idea," she says, and puts Zura's arm through hers. Together they walk down the hall to Zura's room. Nana points to the bed. "How about we bring your favorite quilt to class? These quilt patterns come from another long-ago tradition. Even though they are not exactly the same as the marks on my face, they can help explain them. What do you think?"

Zura traces some of the designs she loves with her fingers. When Nana Akua first made the quilt for Zura, she explained that the patterns were *Adinkra* symbols of the Akan people of Ghana. The symbols represent more than fifty important qualities, like wisdom and creativity.

Zura wishes the marks were only on the quilt and not on Nana Akua's face. Still, she says, "Okay, we can bring it."

On Grandparents Day, Zura wears one of her African dresses sewn by Nana. And Nana Akua looks especially regal in her bright-patterned *kaba* with matching skirt and head wrap.

There are lots of oohs and aahs when they arrive.

The classroom is decorated with a rainbow of balloons that float up to the ceiling. There are large welcome signs made with colored markers.

A tall chair is on the rug for the
grandparents to sit in when they speak.

First is Alejo's *abuelo,* who passes around photos of
the biggest bluefish he ever caught.
Next, Bisou's mimi shows the class a video called
"Mr. Cavity and the Magic Toothbrush."

And then Lester's grandparents, who owned a barbershop for many years, hold up matching clippers. "Anybody need a haircut?" they ask, laughing.

Finally, it's Nana Akua's turn. She sits in the special grandparent chair, with Zura next to her. Zura clutches her quilt tightly, and her voice shakes when she gives her introduction. "This is my Nana Akua, and she is from Ghana, a country in West Africa."

WELCOME

Nana Akua squeezes Zura's shoulder and starts talking.

"Hello, children. I'm sure you noticed the marks on my face. Has anyone seen anything like them before?"

"No," say all the children.

"These marks were gifts from my parents, who were happy and proud that I was born," she continues. "I am likewise proud to wear them. Most Ghanaian parents don't celebrate in this way anymore, but it was once an important tradition."

Zura watches, her eyes wide as cups, as Nana Akua walks slowly around the circle so everyone can see her face up close.

"It's interesting," she says, "that in this country I often notice people who put tattoos on their body that have special meanings."

"Yours are way better than tattoos," Theodore says. "Because they grew up with you."

Nana Akua smiles. "Why, thank you, young man," she says. "And I brought some special makeup so that each of you can have beautiful African symbols on your faces, too. The kind that wash off! My expert helper will hold up her quilt, which shows some symbols you can choose from."

The other students look at Zura expectantly. She unfolds the quilt with care. "Today I'm going to choose the *bese saka* symbol. It looks like a flower, and my nana told me it stands for power and unity."

Nana Akua paints the symbol onto
Zura's cheek in gold while Zura holds
very still. The other children clap
when it's all done.

"Come and choose your favorite
symbol," Zura says to them.

Alejo, who wants to be a beatboxer, points to the *hwemudua* symbol because he thinks it looks like a keyboard. Nana Akua tells him it means "high quality and excellence."

Bisou wants to be a veterinarian and picks the *denkyem* symbol, which is shaped like a crocodile, one of her favorite animals. It stands for cleverness.

Peter and Inez decide on the *adwo* symbol, which looks like the inside of a sliced apple with two identical halves. "Twins, like us," Peter says. Nana says the symbol means "peace and quiet."

"Like Mommy and Daddy say we never give them!" Inez shouts.

Nana Akua paints and paints until every child
has their own design. The other grandparents
choose symbols for themselves, too.

Zura's face glows as she watches Nana Akua fold up her quilt to go home.

And this time it's Zura who gives her very special, not-like-anyone-else's nana one of those big hugs, the kind that wrap around you like a sweater.

GLOSSARY

abuelo (ah-BWAY-lo): Spanish word for "grandfather."

Adinkra (ah-DINK-ra): A group of symbols, originating hundreds of years ago in Côte d'Ivoire, that tell stories and teach lessons. The symbols appear on pottery, jewelry, and other decorative items, including fabrics initially once worn only by African leaders but now worn by many people, both in African countries and in other places in the world. *Adinkra* also means "goodbye" in Twi, a Ghanaian language spoken by the Ashanti tribe.

Akua (ah-KOO-ah): A female Ghanaian name meaning "born on Wednesday."

Ashanti (ah-SHAN-tee): A major ethnic group living in central Ghana.

djembe (JEM-bay): Bambara (a language spoken in Mali) word for a West African rope-tuned drum played with one's bare hands.

kaba (KAH-bah): A traditional Ghanaian woman's top, usually worn over a long skirt or fabric tied around the waist.

maame (MAH-mee): Twi word for "mother."

Mimi (mee-mee): In Hebrew, the pet form of the name Miryam, and sometimes a nickname for "Grandmother."

paapa (PAH-pa): Twi for "father."

SOURCES

West African Wisdom: Adinkra Symbols & Meanings: adinkra.org

Adinkra Brand African Knowledge Hub: adinkrabrand.com/knowledge-hub

Adinkra Symbols with Meanings: adinkrasymbols.org

Willis, W. Bruce. *The Adinkra Dictionary: A Visual Primer on the Language of Adinkra*. Pyramid Complex, 1998.

ACKNOWLEDGMENTS

I owe many debts of gratitude to: my husband, Chuck, and my children, Justin, Elam, and Nile; the early readers of my book; my brilliant agent, Regina Brooks; my visionary editor, Anne Schwartz; my cocreator, illustrator April Harrison, who gave my characters beating hearts; my friend and shero, Magdalene Awuah, who shared her wisdom and culture; others who have documented and preserved the rich Ashanti traditions online and in books; and the Writers' Room of Boston, where much of this story was written. —T.E.W.

ADINKRA SYMBOLS AND THEIR MEANINGS

**aban
(ah-BAHN):**
two-storied house;
means "authority and power"

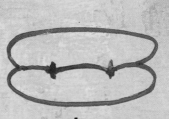

**adinkrahene
(ah-DIN-krah-heh-nee):**
chief of Adinkra symbols;
means "leadership and greatness"

**adwo
(AH-jo):**
calmness;
means "peace and quiet"

ahoden (ah-ho-DEN):
energy;
means "energy and strength"

**akoko nan
(AH-ko-ko NINE):**
hen's leg;
means "patience and discipline"

**akoma
(ah-ko-MAH):**
heart;
means "love and patience"

**bese saka
(beh-see SAH-kah):**
bunch of cola nuts;
means "power and unity."

**boafo ye na
(bo-AH-foo yay NAH):**
support;
means "willing helper"

denkyem (den-CHEM):
crocodile;
means "cleverness"

**duafe
(doo-AH-fah):**
wooden comb;
means "beauty and care"